Designed by Flowerpot Press
in Franklin, TN.
www.FlowerpotPress.com
Designer: Stephanie Meyers
Editor: Katrine Crow
DJS-0912-0161
ISBN: 978-1-4867-1201-4
Made in China/Fabriqué en Chine

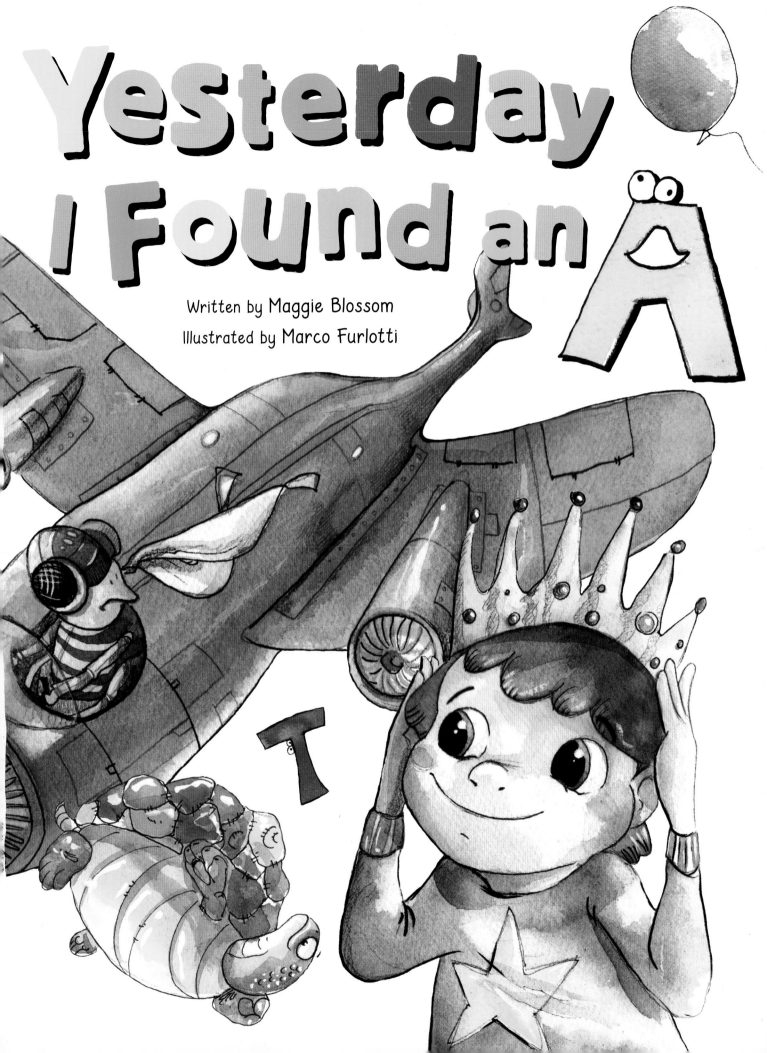

# Yesterday I Found an A

Written by Maggie Blossom

Illustrated by Marco Furlotti

Yesterday I was home alone, calm and quiet as a mouse,
when suddenly I heard a noise from somewhere in the house.

I went to my closet and opened it wide,
curious to see what was hiding inside...

That's when yesterday I found an **A** in the closet right here in my room.
And out rolled some apples, an accordion, and an airplane zipping by...zoooom!

And that made me nervous that things might go wrong.
What if the rest of the letters had all tagged along?

What if **B** brought some butterflies, a bear, and a bee, and a billion balloons as a present for me?

Or if **C** came with a cat, and a clock, and a clown,
and we formed a cool club, and they gave me a crown?

What if **D** brought a daisy to deliver good luck
and a dinosaur dancing to a drum-drumming duck?

And if then in danced an elephant, spry as can be,
who said she was here as a guest of the **E**?
And if the **E** also brought eight excited eggs,
who all flittered about the poor elephant's legs?

What if **F** and its friends left footprints on the floor,
and I followed them and five frogs and four fish out the door?

What if I found the **G** in the very next room
with a goose and a gander dressed as bride and groom?

And the **H** was hopping onto a huge hobbyhorse,
dressed for the wedding with a top hat, of course!

What if the I invited an inchworm along for the fun,
and they ate all the ice cream until it was done?

What if the J just jumped in with a jelly bean game,
and then a jack-in-the-box ate them all when he came?

What if **K** came along with a kangaroo and her kid?

And if **L** let a lion slide through on a lid?

Would you mind if the **M** also showed up that day
with a marvelous monkey with music to play?

Or if **N** noticed nothing but just wandered along
counting the nine notes in that monkey's nice song?

What if **0** and an octopus both came in at that time,
and the octopus was writing an orange's rhyme?

And as it was writing, the octopus was struggling,
trying to make rhymes from the words it was juggling.

"This is hard," said the octopus.
"Nothing rhymes with orange..."

ORDER

OUT

ORANGE

OBOE

What if in paraded **P** with the prettiest pig you've ever seen,
followed quite closely by a **Q** and a queen?

And if the queen needed the **R** to roll out her red rug,
and her robot to straighten things out with a tug?

What if **S** sauntered in with a snake six feet tall
and a smiling, swinging soldier who soared over us all?

What if **T** trotted in with twin teddies in girdles
to enjoy the tumbling tricks of three cute patchwork turtles?

And if **U** brought a big ukulele to play,
and it rocked up and down in an umbrella all day?

What if our vacuum went vrrrooooom...and gave **V** a chase,
and it snagged on some velvet and knocked down a vase?

And if then **W** waltzed in acting wacky and wild,
while a great big blue whale drank our water and smiled?

What if **X** brought a xylophone that made a nice sound,
as **Y**'s yak and **Z**'s zebra both danced all around?

What if this all happened? What if it were true?
What would I say? What would you do?

I guess I would just have to tell you this story.
Then we'd clean up this mess, and I'd tell you "I'm sorry,
but when yesterday I found an **A** and it brought **B** through **Z**,
they made a great big mess in here, and it had nothing to do with me!"